Is it *really* possible to write a complete short story using only 55 words?

"Absolutely fascinating!

These little gems are everything their editor says they are—and much more. [They're] imaginative, poignant, funny, surprising, thought provoking, clever, meaningful, and even, yes, experimental. Anyone who wants to write should try to match these and learn. Amazing—and fun!"

Michael Collins

"Many excited my imagination. It's not easy to wrap a complete story in so few words.

The surprise is that it is done so well so often."

Larry Niven

"The perfect literary form for the 1990s!

They offer drama, suspense, comedy, and horror, and all in less than a minute. Sorta like sex (Wait a minute—did I say that?)"

Christopher Moore

"Your Fifty-Five Fiction contest gave my writing students the motivation to brainstorm, edit, revise, and then write final drafts. Particularly challenging was the word limit.

It makes for a great lesson in character, setting, plot, conflict, and resolution!"

Mike Bland

"These short stories are nothing short of amazing!

I betcha can't read just one!"

Brandy Brandon

Try writing one yourself! See page 231!

55
fiction

The World's
Shortest Stories

The World's

Compiled and Edited by
Steve Moss

Illustrations by
Glen Starkey

New Times Press, San Luis Obispo
John Daniel and Company, Santa Barbara

55 fiction ℠

Shortest Stories

Published by
New Times Press
and
John Daniel and Company

Distributed to the trade by
Daniel & Daniel, Publishers, Inc.
Post Office Box 21922
Santa Barbara, Calif. 93121

Design: Alex Zuniga
Editorial assistance and proofreading: Diane DeRushia Urbani

Typeset in Goudy and Campanile by Adobe Systems, Inc., and
Franklin Gothic Condensed by Fluent Laser

Library of Congress Cataloging-in-Publication Data:

The world's shortest stories / [edited by] Steve Moss
p.   cm.
ISBN 1-880284-11-1
1. Short stories, American.   I. Moss, Steve,   1948-
PS648. S5W67   1995
813'. 0108—dc20

Fifty-Five Fiction is a writing contest held annually by New Times, 197 Santa Rosa St., San Luis Obispo, Calif. 93405. For further information, please contact New Times Press at this address. Most of these stories originally appeared in New Times.

Printed in the United States of America

2   4   6   8   10   9   7   5   3   1

First Edition
April, 1995

For my father, Harry Walter Moss, a man of many words who would nevertheless have enjoyed this book.

———————————————

Special Thanks

To Bev Johnson for believing in me right from the start, and for so much more; and to John Kokot, who got me started one cold winter day in Syracuse, N.Y. (and I don't mean my car). Thanks also to Alex Zuniga, accomplice and art director extraordinaire; and to Roland Sweet, man of many talents—both weird and otherwise—and fearless champion of absurdities everywhere.

Thanks also to Robin Bell for her constant encouragements and gracious help throughout; to Rich Udell of Harcourt Brace Jovanovich, Inc., who took the time to help me lay the groundwork when this was but a fledgling idea; to M. Scott Radovich for his always useful counsel and good humor; to Ken Simon for reasons I can't pinpoint exactly, but who somehow had a hand in all this; and to Dean Christianson and his many talented writing students over the years.

And thanks also to Steve Rupp and Diane Urbani for their comments and suggestions; to Tim Haggerty for his enthusiasm and confidence when the project began; to Richard Jahnke, who took a chance with me way back when; to Sandy Young and Terry and Penny Davies of the Earthling Bookshop for their years of helpful sponsorships; and to John Daniel for his unhesitating generosity and encouragement, who pointed me in the right direction right when I needed it.

Contents

INTRODUCTION

How short can a story be and still be considered a story? Charles Schulz had an answer to that question several years ago in his "Peanuts" comic strip. Crabby old Lucy was once asked by Linus to please, please, please tell him a story. Lucy grudgingly obliged. Said she: "A man was born. He lived and died. The end."

That's the shortest story I've ever read. But, like Linus, I was left somewhat dissatisfied.

So maybe the question should be asked differently: How short can a story be and still be considered a *good* story? What's the briefest possible narrative that still allows for a satisfying read? I think I've found the answer. And since you're holding this book in your hands right now, that means you have, too.

Consider for a moment that the paragraph you just finished reading contains exactly 55 words. It's an absurdly tiny number. No, it's an *impossibly* tiny number. So how could it allow for any kind of scope or quality? All I know is that's the length of a typical Fifty-Five Fiction story, and that it does. I also know that in the following pages, you'll find murder and suspense, horror and intrigue, love and betrayal, plus distant worlds and inner demons. All in a measly 55 words.

When I announced the first Fifty-Five Fiction contest in the fall of 1987, it was a gamble. I wasn't really sure writers could pull it off. Admittedly, most stories sent to us that year weren't very good, but every now and then a tiny gem would shine up from the typewritten page, submitted by someone who truly understood the genre. I've often tried explaining these 55-word creations to people, but most of them think I'm crazy. Now I have this book to show them, a collection culled from the top stories sent to us over the years.

If you've already glanced through these pages, you know what I'm talking about. You've probably also noticed that many stories have something in common besides their stingy word count: the surprise ending. Many writers have sensed that with so little to work with, the successful Fifty-Five Fiction short story demands something extra to create a satisfying payoff, and they have plotted their tales accordingly.

The famous "Twilight Zone" episode featuring Burgess

Meredith as a bespectacled bookworm who finds himself the sole survivor of a nuclear holocaust, and who breaks his glasses amidst books aplenty, could easily have been written as a Fifty-Five Fiction story.

Fifty-Five Fiction is storytelling at its very leanest, where each word is chosen with utmost care on its way to achieving its fullest effect. It's what O. Henry might have conjured up if he'd had only the back of a business card to write upon, or what "The Twilight Zone" would have been like if it were only a minute long. It's H.H. Munro's famous mini-short stories written even smaller.

Fifty-Five Fiction is fanciful and murderous, speculative and absurd, creepy and touching, and just plain wild. But most of all, Fifty-Five Fiction is fun, which is exactly what reading and writing are supposed to be. Writers more accustomed to stretching out leisurely across the page would find their attempts at Fifty-Five Fiction frustrating.

James Michener would have a time of it.

But maybe not. Some who've taken the Fifty-Five Fiction challenge have later said that the discipline of making every word count easily transferred to their longer works, and that this tightly focused exercise in literary minimalism ultimately helped them write more judicious longer prose.

That's why Fifty-Five Fiction shouldn't be viewed as little

more than short-attention-span fiction for the MTV generation. Instead, it's become a jumping-off point for new fiction writers testing the waters of their imaginations when the water (not to mention that empty page in front of them) seems vast and intimidating. Many who began writing Fifty-Five Fiction have gone on to successfully tackle much longer stories. I'd like to think at least one of them is now finishing up a first novel—and that it's 555 pages long.

The challenge of Fifty-Five Fiction can be daunting. Paring plot and narrative down to their utter essences and thinking hard about each word and judging its appropriateness are part of the Fifty-Five Fiction process. It's difficult to describe to non-writers the intellectual joy of the effort, the emotional rush of creating something small, orderly, and beautiful out of absolutely nothing.

When O. Henry finished writing "The Gift of the Magi," he must have felt something similar. No doubt H.H. Munro did, too, when he completed his classic mini-story, "The Open Window."

One thing I didn't expect was that writing instructors would take a fancy to Fifty-Five Fiction. But they have. I've received letters of praise—and hundreds of student samples—from both high school and college teachers who've been using it regularly and enthusiastically over the years. One creative-writing teacher put it this way: "The students have learned word economy, editing skills, and the basic essentials of the short story in a very simple and easy-to-take manner. And to top it off, it was fun."

But would Linus have been satisfied after reading a Fifty-Five Fiction story? Does such a stingy word count allow for a really satisfying read? You already know what I think.

As James Thomas—whose stories had a limit of 750 words—said in the introduction to his "Flash Fiction" anthology (W.W. Norton & Co.), "Like all fiction that matters, their success depends not on their length, but on their depth, their clarity of vision, their human significance—the extent to which the reader can recognize in them the real stuff of real life."

I don't think I could say it any better.

All I know is that Fifty-Five Fiction writers say it shorter.

Steve Moss
San Luis Obispo, Calif.
1995

WITH
MURDER
IN MIND

Bedtime Story

"Careful, honey, it's loaded," he said, re-entering the bedroom.

Her back rested against the headboard. "This for your wife?"

"No. Too chancy. I'm hiring a professional."

"How about me?"

He smirked. "Cute. But who'd be dumb enough to hire a lady hit man?"

She wet her lips, sighting along the barrel. "Your wife."

Jeffrey Whitmore

Accidents

Reginald Cooke had buried three wives before he married Cecile Northwood.

"Tragic accidents," he told her.

"How sad," replied Cecile. "Were they...wealthy?"

"And beautiful," said Reginald.

They honeymooned in the Alps.

Later, Cecile told her new husband, "You know, darling, my first husband died in a tragic mountaineering accident."

"How sad," replied Justin Marlow.

Mark Cohen

Murder Must Advertise

Seaside adventurer seeks female for candlelit dinner...

Shivering with anticipation, Laura enters the secluded beach estate. She rings. The door swings open...

By candlelight, piranhas jerk and devour the last chunks of flesh and blond hair.

"That's nineteen," coos Lucretia, applying Laura's burgundy lipstick. "My new wardrobe'll kill 'em!"

Female, murderously fashionable, seeks adventuresome male...

L. J. Barnett

Dusk to Dawn

Dawn breaks
in two.
Damn.
I liked Dawn. Nice girl. Weak
back, though.
Oh, well.
Have to bury her somewhere. In
the basement, maybe?
What's that?
Dusk arrives. She's early.
Too early. Have to kill her too.
Too bad.
Nice girl.
Guess I'll be busy tonight.
From Dusk to Dawn.

Bruce Harmor

Death and Denouement

"Pretty grisly, eh Jacques?"

"Sickening. Any angles?"

"Well, a pattern does seem to be emerging, lieutenant. Yesterday, homicide found a copy of *Death of a Salesman* at the murder site; today, some nut goes and whacks this Fuller Brush guy."

"Great. A literary serial killer. Find any books?"

"Yes...*The French Lieutenant's Woman*, sir."

Joe Hubbell

The Understudy

"The show must go on," said the director when the star dropped dead moments before act one. The star, not the understudy, would play the corpse tonight.

The understudy changed quickly. His performance was inspired. The star was flawless in his final role.

The understudy, fingering the syringe in his pocket, bowed to thunderous applause.

Sheree Pellemier

Death in the Afternoon

"Come out from behind the tree, Louie, so I can spray your brains all over."

"You don't have the guts to pull the trigger."

"I've got more guts than you're gonna have brains."

"You've got peanuts for brains, Tony."

Bang!

"...and another!"

Bang!

"Louis! Tony! Supper!"

"Comin', Mom!"

Priscilla Mintling

At the Canyon

The newlywed heiress oozed, "Poopsy, the sign reads, 'Clairvoyant Canyon. Call Out a Question. Wait for Answering Echoes.'"

Overhanging a guardrail, she called, "Does he love me?"

"—Does he? Does he?" came the echo.

Discomfited, she tried again. "Is unhappiness behind me?"

"—Behind you, behind you—" it prognosticated, just before her new beneficiary shoved.

Curt Homan

Sorry I Asked

"It's a dark night, honey."

She whirled to meet the tall man trapping her against her car.

"So what do you do, baby?"

Her arm slashed a silver arc to his throat. His shriek became a gurgle.

She flung the scalpel on the floorboard, and driving away, said to the writhing figure: "I'm a surgeon."

W.D. Miller

Out of the Fog

Lyn clutched her purse as footsteps approached along the fog-shrouded lane. Emily, a fellow prostitute, emerged.

"Any business?" asked Lyn.

Emily shrugged. "Some. And you?"

"Not yet, tonight."

"'Tis slow because of The Ripper," Emily sighed. "Seems everyone's afraid of Jack."

"Actually, the full name's 'Jacquelyn,'" Lyn said, pulling the knife from her purse.

Curt Homan

One Rainy Night

Rain obscured the Georgia country road. Jody, driving a stolen truck, braked suddenly for a white-uniformed hitchhiker who climbed into the cab gasping, "My car broke down!"

"You a doctor?"

"Right."

"The asylum?" asked criminally insane Jody, who'd just fled from there.

"Yes," lied murderous William, who'd just escaped from prison.

Dolorez Roupe

The Mystery

"You needn't look so smug, Watson."

"Sorry, Holmes. It's just that I believe you're finally stumped. You'll never unravel this crime."

Holmes stood up and gestured emphatically with the stem of his pipe.

"I'm afraid you're wrong. I do know who killed Mrs. Worthington."

"Incredible! No witnesses! No clues! Who did it?"

"I did, Watson."

Tom Ford

Into the Night

Look, smile, teeth, lips, voice, sexy, car, feel, apartment, couch, music, dance, lights, drink, moist, dry, soft, firm, fast, slow, easy, hard, leg, knee, thigh, shoulders, breast, fingers, silky, rough, breath, living room, bedroom, bathroom, kitchen, basement, bed, pillow, sheets, shower, cigarette, coffee, stockings, brassiere, dress, shirt, naked, rattle, door, husband, scramble, kill, clothes, window.

Dick Skeen

Gourmet Comestibles

Wealthy Mrs. Wigelsworth's eyes gleamed when she ordered tender fillet of filly from Pat R. Hamm, proprietor of Gourmet Comestibles, for a dinner party honoring the police chief.

When her daughter didn't show up, the chief promised to find her. He did.

Mr. Hamm was arrested.

The chief had indigestion.

Mrs. Wigelsworth became a vegetarian.

Dolorez Roupe

December 8, 1980, 5:59 p.m.

She closed the history book and sighed.

"That General Custer. He should *never* have left the safety of the Dakota territory."

He was in too much of a hurry to listen. He picked up his guitar and headed for the door.

"Bloody hell, Yoko. Let's *go*. We're going to be late."

David Congalton

Final Witness

Pandemonium erupted. The next witness was walking through the courtroom doors.

"Order in the court!" the judge bellowed, cracking his gavel.

All eyes focused on Tommy, who was sitting on the stand, his mouth open in shock.

It was quite obvious now who'd murdered his wife.

No one.

Candice C. Mutschler

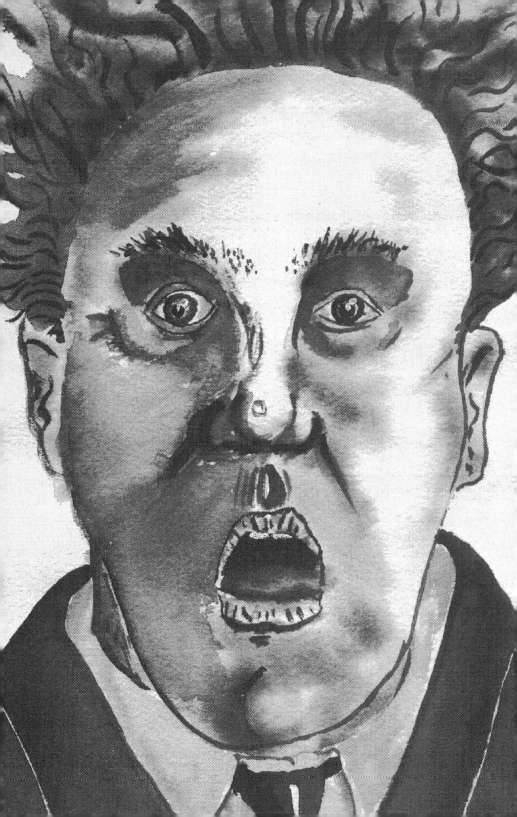

Malice Aforethought

"You stuck him good, Zack. Right between the ribs. Beautiful." Bobby shifted, wincing as the handcuffs pinched.

"Whaddya mean, *I* stuck him?" grunted Zack, his knees pressed against the cage. "I tried to stop *you!*"

"Why, you filthy liar—"

The officer peered into his rear-view mirror. "Hey, pal, who you talkin' to back there?"

Mike Phillips

Grandma Meets the Ax Murderer

The crazed ax-murderer approached the house. Having ravaged the entire neighborhood, his sack of booty was almost full.

Alone inside, the old woman sat knitting. The murderer raised his blood-stained ax and rang the porch doorbell. Slowly, she opened the door and peered into his face.

"Trick or treat!" the little boy shouted.

Diane Elliott

Roadkill

"**H**ey, Dad, I'm joining a *scavenger* hunt tonight!"

"Sounds fun, son."

"There's a rumor we'll have to find at least one *roadkill!*"

"A roadkill? Gross!"

"So could I borrow the car?"

"…Okay."

"Dad, it's so nice out this evening, you oughta go for a *walk!*"

"…Hmmm. Think I will. See you later."

"*For sure!*"

Spinny Bazookawitz

The Window

Since his Rita's brutal murder, Carter sits at the window.

No television, reading, correspondence. His life is whatever passes outside those curtains.

He doesn't care to leave the room, or know who furnishes meals, pays bills. His world is joggers, changing seasons, passing cars, Rita's ghost.

Carter doesn't realize padded cells don't have windows.

Jane Orvis

On the Bus

Where does she get off not allowing her eyes to meet mine? Why this childish game? Everyone on the bus is watching.

Where does she get off ignoring that "certain something" between us? She'll learn the price when I follow her home.

Where does she get off thinking she's too good for me?

Sixteenth Avenue.

Jane Orvis

The Magician and His Assistant

Carmine the Magnificent could not believe Nina was cheating on him. Filled with anger, he planned his revenge.

Nina crawled into the box on stage for their finale. Carmine the Magnificent was indeed magnificent as he worked his magic. When the last sword pierced the box, there was a cold shriek.

"Abra-cadaver!" exclaimed Carmine.

Martha Jara

I Want to Report an Accident

"Celia, it's all your fault. You'll find my bloated body in the pool. Farewell. Umberto."

She stumbled out, the note in her fist, and saw me, floating face down, like a giant fly marooned in Jell-O.

When she leapt to rescue me, and remembered she couldn't swim, I got out.

—Convict 338412

Tom Ford

Windigo

Outside the blizzard raged, while inside the fire hissed and popped. He sat watching the flames dance.

Frozen they found him with dismembered limbs stacked neatly in the fireplace.

In darkened rooms above lay the bodies of his wife and children. Crimson-orbed eyes of Windigo, the essence of madness, glowed faintly in the shadows.

Larry J. Juhl

Split Personality

He was gorgeous. She was thrilled. But puzzled.

"Why were your other relationships so short?" she wondered aloud as they walked.

He glanced upward.

"Well, I have this slight problem..."

Later, the detective grimaced at the ghastly sight of the young girl, bloody beneath the full moon.

In the distance, a wolf howled.

Mark Turner

Mindy

"Walk you out, Mindy?"

"No thanks, I'll be okay."

At her car, an elderly lady asked for help.

"Honey, my jumper cables are in the back seat."

Mindy couldn't find them.

"You sure they're here?"

A man's voice answered.

"No...but you are."

The guard never noticed the silver wig in the empty parking lot.

Phil Nash
Joe Hubbell

Hide and Seek

"...Ninety-nine, one hundred! Ready or not, here I come!"

I hate being "it," but always find them easier. Entering a darkened room, I whisper to the hiders there, "Olly, olly, oxen free..."

They follow me home, down mirrored corridors where, too often, I see the black cowl and scythe of my own reflection.

Curt Homan

Blood Sure

"Can you keep a secret, Em?"

"Sure."

"Blood sure?"

"Look, Ty—"

"Oh, I forgot. *Doctor.* Ever since you left the holler, you's better'n us kinfolk and our ways."

Emmett sighed, then extended his palm. He winced as his brother's blade grew red.

"What secret?"

Blood trickled from between their thumbs.

"Em...I gots AIDS, man."

Joe Hubbell

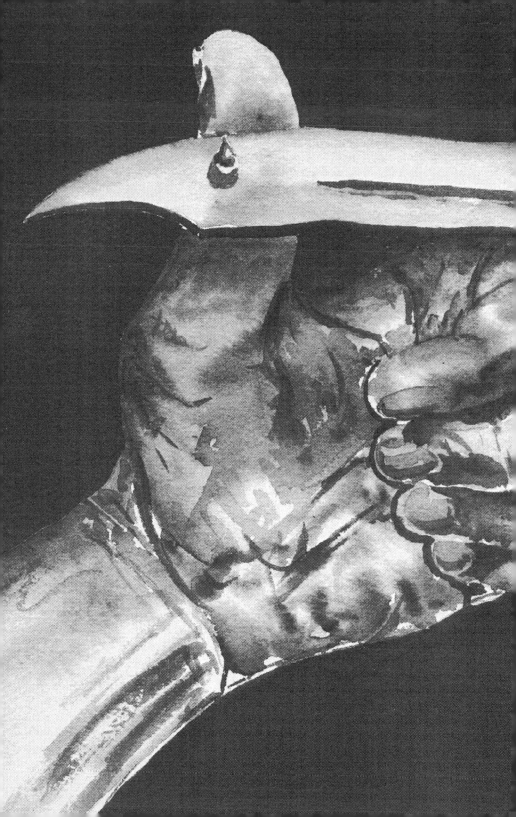

Bird Talk

"Henry," mimed the parrot as the two policemen considered the body sprawled in the pool of blood.

"Henry, no," squawked the bird.

One officer walked to the desk and glanced at the dead man's appointment book. "$$$" encircled "9:30 a.m."

"Henry—*don't!*" shrieked the parrot.

"So how many Henrys this guy know?"

"Just one."

Scott D. Shaw

A Break in the Case

"Eight stab wounds, eight corpses, zero clues," sighed the inspector, driving through the night rain. "He's neat, efficient."

The criminologist polished his glasses. "Yes. Also slight, left-handed, myopic. Loves Beethoven. And I know his whereabouts."

Screech of brakes.

"Where?" cried the inspector.

"Here," said the other, grinning hugely as he slammed home the blade.

William E. Blundell

That Settles That

Tom was a handsome, fun-loving young man, albeit a bit drunk when he got into the argument with Sam, his roommate of just two months.

"You can't. You can *not* write a short story in just 55 words, you idiot!"

Sam shot him dead on the spot.

"Oh, yes you can," Sam said, smiling.

Terry L. Tilton

YES,
LOVE
HAPPENS

On the Rebound

"Why?"

"It's over, Angela. Done."

"But I *need* you!"

"Needed me," George corrected.

"I'll *die* without you!"

George patted her hand. "You'll live, dear girl. Rather, knowing you, I'd say...thrive."

He stood, kissed her, was gone.

Sniffling, Angela watched him pass their waiter. So handsome! She hadn't noticed.

"Excuse...me?" she called shyly.

Mary Beth Hennessy

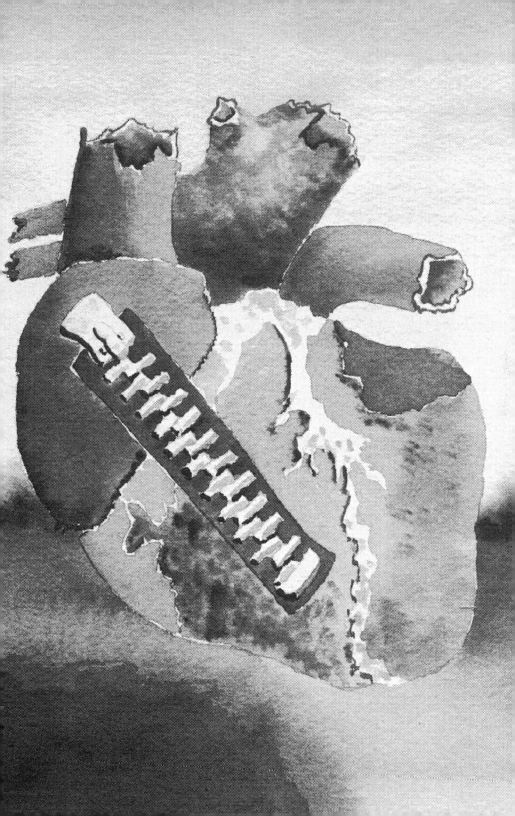

The Affair

"Roses are red, violets are blue. I hate your husband and so do you. Meet me at eight."

Sarah tore the note up.

"Hey, what's that?" Stu asked.

"Notes for tonight's meeting."

"You been goin' to *lots* of them things lately," he sneered. "What's it tonight? Savin' the goddamn whales?"

"No," she smiled. "Population control."

Suzanne Caplette Champeau

Winning Jane

Jeff loved Jane. Cliff threatened mayhem if anyone approached Jane.

Perfect!

Jeff waited until Cliff started bragging to someone about his football triumphs. Then Jeff brought Jane some punch and complimented her dress.

Cliff hit him. Jane mopped the punch off Jeff and told Cliff her opinion of bullies and jerks.

Jeff drove Jane home.

Barbara Wray Wayland

The Dream

As a child, she dreamt of wolves. They chased her each night for one year. She ran and was never caught.

Later, she met a man. Playful and protective. Sharp teeth, soft fur.

She still dreams of wolves.

But now, as they lope through her dreams, she runs with them.

Sheree Pellemeier

The Beginning

The phone rang again. She closed her eyes and sighed.

Part of her wanted to give in to his adulterous fantasy. She twisted the gold ring on her finger and looked at the clock. Bob wouldn't be home until eleven. She slowly picked up the receiver.

"Once," she said to him. "But never again."

David de Vos

A Pilgrim's Tale

He entered sheepishly and knelt at his wife's bedside.

"Priscilla, dearest, she meant nothing to me! Can you ever forgive me?"

She was flushed. "Yes, John. Love is forgiveness."

"Angel!" He kissed her forehead, grabbed his musket, and left, slamming the front door.

Priscilla leaned over the bed's edge to peer beneath.

"Miles," she beckoned.

Curt Homan

The Salon Visit

"Anyway," the woman in the chair continued, "his wife's so *gullible!* Bill always says he's going bowling; she *always* believes him!"

The beautician smiled. "My husband William loves bowling."

Never used to…Goes all the time now… She paused, frowning.

Then a slow, bitter smile emerged. "Let's start on your perm. You're gonna look *unforgettable.*"

Elizabeth Eula

Lounge Angel

Bart choked on his Corona when two female legs disappeared beneath his table.

Glorious lips spoke:

"What do you do?"

He sold cars.

"I produce Broadway plays."

"Oh—I'd hoped you were this beautiful dreamer I once met on a car lot," she said, leaving.

He called work.

Quit.

And followed her into the night.

Rusty Evans

Young Love

The lovers found the genie's lamp on the beach.

"For freeing me," said the genie, "I will grant you each a wish."

Looking into the boy's eyes, the girl said, "I wish we could be lovers until the end of the world."

Looking out to sea, the boy said, "I wish the world would end."

David W. Meyers

Werling

Werling Werner was witless. Without worrying whether wife Wilma was working, Werling wasted wampum willfully. Worthless Werling was workless. When Werling woke wondering what wife Wilma was wanting, we wondered why Werling wanted women. Werling was without wisdom. Women want warmth. Wilma was wet. Werling Werner's weenie was worthless. Wilma went without. Woe was Werling.

Glen Starkey

A Second Chance

His love had gone. In despair, he flung himself off the Golden Gate Bridge.

Coincidentally, a few yards away, a girl made her own suicide plunge.

The two passed in midair.

Their eyes met.

Their chemistry clicked.

It was true love.

They realized it.

Three feet above the water.

Jay Bonestell

Rites of Passage

He'd known her since she was very young. She was the most beautiful girl in the world, and he loved her deeply. At one time he had been her idol. Now he was losing her to another man.

Eyes glistening, he kissed her cheek softly, then smiled as he gave her away to the groom.

Mark Turner

The Old and the Restless

Mom, 76 and alone, suddenly decided to visit Europe. With Jean, she told us.

My brother and I thought, okay—we can railroad Mom into Happy Haven as planned, later.

Meanwhile, we roamed the vast estate, happily discussing arrangements.

Then came the postcard.

"Marrying Gene in Paris! He's only 64 and a *doll!* Love, Mom."

Anne G. Phillips

At an Apeeling Party

He refused to be married without her. He checked his watch again.

"You think she'll come?"

"Sure, I spoke to her answering machine."

He paced. "I'm only doing this once. She'd better show."

"Relax, she'll make it."

Then they heard cheers and whistles outside.

The stripper entered, smiling.

"Hi, guys!"

The bachelor party could begin.

Damon Younger

The Once and Future Beach

"Oh, mama," Larry said. "Look at that *babe*."

"Perfectly shaped breasts," said Jim.

"And what a tan!"

"God, I love girls in bikinis."

A bronzed college boy lying nearby whispered, "Jerry, listen to those fat old guys."

"Yeah...guess they've got nothing better to do than—oh, mama, Tim, would you look at that *babe*."

Edward E. Goto

Rendezvous

The phone rang.

"Hello," she whispered.

"Victoria, it's me. Meet me by the dock at midnight."

"I'll be there, sweetheart."

"And don't forget the bubbly, babe," he said.

"I won't, darling. I want you tonight."

"I can't wait!" he said, and hung up.

She sighed, then smiled.

"I wonder who that was," she said.

Nichole Weddle

Like Two Ships

He entered the elevator.

"Ground floor, please," he said.

He sounds nice, she thought, but he wouldn't notice me.

He noticed. He noticed her standing there, eyes straight ahead. But he didn't blame her.

Nice perfume, he thought as they parted, he lightly stroking his disfigured face, she counting the steps to the waiting van.

Chris Macy

The Dance

He shuffles to my locker. Skinny Steve with the zits. Yuck! Probably wants to ask me to the dance. My last chance. Oh, well. Better than being a wallflower, like Jenny.

Deep breath. "Hi, Steve."

"Hi, Sue."

"You wanted to ask me something?"

Even his zits blushed.

"I wondered...do you have Jenny's phone number?"

Joy Jolissaint

Master Thief

Coins. Nickels, pennies, shining dollars. Inspecting purses, browsing pockets, poking couches. Everything moves from my long fingers into my deep pockets.

Fell in love once. Beautiful meter maid. Begged her to stay. She awoke first; cleaned me out. Boxes of quarters, bags of dimes. Left a note.

"Baby, collecting's my life. Never could change."

Catherine E. McDonald

Winds of Change

On the South Wind, she came into his heart. From the West Wind, he learned about her mind. The East Wind taught him of her spirit.

Then the weather changed and all the winds blew at once, creating a great, rising circular storm, and she left him on the North Wind, his heart covered with ice.

Richard M. Sharp

Just Desserts

Martha hungered for sex, not a sundae. At 300 pounds, she'd been settling for too little. Sighing, she closed the menu.

The very thin man saw this and approached.

He explained that since he'd stopped having sex, he couldn't eat.

She said that since she'd not, she couldn't stop.

They left together in anticipatory bliss.

Rebecca L. Conner

Left at the Altar

Oscar, shy to the bone, yet determined to make Bertha his wife, kneeled on his wooden leg, asking, "Will you be mine?"

Bertha, rubbing his leg with a sandpaper sheet, answered, "Only if you'll get this thing varnished for the wedding."

Later, when asked why he didn't marry Bertha, Oscar answered, "Because I didn't lacquer."

Donald G. Wallace

A Photographer's Regrets

Looking back now, I see you swaddled in white sheets, your hair hopelessly tangled and your necklace faintly glinting gold between your breasts. Telltale picture; the manifest image of all my desires in sharp focus and staring back at me.

God, how I wish I'd never tripped the shutter.

Sometimes it's better to forget.

D. Boon

Love

Brenda promised the horizontal hokey-pokey if he wore a chicken suit and spoke French. Wayne sewed and studied for six months.

Knocking on her door, he was one sharp bird who could conjugate like a Parisian in heat.

Brenda greeted him with the news she was now into vegetables and Swahili.

Love is cruel.

Daniel J. Eggert

Galileo

It was another sun-drenched day at the Cove.

She was definitely a California girl. Blonde, beautiful, tanned.

She had freckles, as the midnight sky has constellations. On her right thigh, the Pleiades. On her left, Orion's belt. The Milky Way was splashed across her shoulders and face.

And he longed to be an astronaut.

Tim Hartwig

You Can Never Go Back

Five years ago she plucked a dandelion and a bindweed blossom from the grass at the mobile home park. Now they're pressed between the pages of an old Moffat's Bible marking the 23rd Psalm.

She never thinks about that day she handed him the tiny flowers. He can never forget.

Jay Bonestell

Two Nights That Pass in the Chips

A second night that week they pushed their carts into opposite ends of the "Chips and Dips" aisle.

As they neared, their prepared conversational gambits dissolved into mutual diffidence.

He pretended interest in chips; she feigned absorption in dips.

They passed in silence.

Glancing over their shoulders, both thought hopelessly: Next week, "Vegetables."

Curt Homan

Moment
of Decision

She could almost hear the prison door clanging shut.

Freedom would be gone forever, control of her own destiny gone, never to return.

Wild thoughts of flight flashed through her mind. But she knew there was no escape.

She turned to the groom with a smile and repeated the words, "I do."

Tina Milburn

Schatchen

"I can find my own dates," Aaron remembered saying.

Playing matchmaker had been his mother's only fault. He winced now as dirt hit her coffin.

Who's that beautiful redhead...a friend of Mom's?

Tess would have come to the funeral even without the promise she'd made to the dying woman she'd nursed during her final days.

Annette Amir

Kim

Our first-grade class raced across the grassy field during recess. Kim with the pretty smile and the golden ponytail and I were fast.

Once we raced across her yard. I don't remember who won.

Kim died a few years later of some disease that I couldn't pronounce.

I run with Kim, even now.

Robert M. Dominguez

Now

Sandra towel-dried her hair on the veranda. The briny smell of the ocean lingered in the breeze.

Inside, the shower was still running. She thought about Pete and the kids. That life seemed years ago. Wasn't that the American dream? Would they understand?

"I loved watching you swim," said Kathy, handing Sandra the hairbrush.

Rae Silver

Smell
the Roses

Wedding fever. Invitations mailed. But he's acting strange. Then, a quarrel. He says it's over. Tells her to go. Tearfully, she writes cancellations.

"But, why?" she asks. "Why?"

A week passes. And another. She misses him terribly. She goes to his apartment and knocks.

She hears his voice. "Hey, Honey, answer the door, will ya?"

Mary Zender

The Wish

The evening glow behind the fog faded as the two walked the almost-deserted beach.

"I'll never understand women."

"Do you really *want* to?"

"Yes, I do. I truly do."

"Oh, all right."

She whispered into his ear; understanding crystallized in his eyes like broken glass.

He ran screaming into the night.

Ross Parsons

In the Garden

Standing there in the garden, she saw him running toward her.

"Tina! My flower! The love of my life!"

He'd said it at last.

"Oh, *Tom!*"

"Tina, my flower!"

"Oh, Tom! I love you, *too!*"

Tom reached her, knelt down, and quickly pushed her aside.

"My *flower!* You were standing on my prize-winning *rose!*"

Hope A. Torres

A Brief Intermission

He was young, Hispanic, handsome, and macho.

She was white, Protestant, divorced, and on the cusp of hormonal decline.

They worked in the kitchen of a luxury hotel and made quick sex inside the pantry during wedding banquets.

Afterward, her thighs would slip past each other as she served up trays of steamed oysters.

Iris Alexandra

For Him and the 3 a.m. Darkness

"I'm drowning."

"You're not. You're safe."

"I'm falling."

"No."

And we lay in the silences, his voice rambling in the surrounding darkness, miles away, until I fell asleep once more.

In the morning, I was alone. I cradled the phone in my arms and tried to find him again.

Kimberly A. Hannah

SWF, A

Seeking

how abou

also, loo

for frien

First Encounter

She had reservations. Lots of them. She thought the personal ads were for losers. But she was terribly lonely and maybe, just maybe...

She placed the ad. The most promising answer arrived early. And now, here she was, waiting at the restaurant for a stranger with a rose in his lapel.

"Daddy? Is that you?"

Arthur L. Willard

Fast Talker

"Fifty-five," she whispered to him.
"Fifty-five miles per hour?"

"No, *words!* That's all we've *got!* Hurry! *Please!*"

Perspiration trickled down his neck; he stepped harder on the accelerator.

"But...there's so *much* I want to tell you! So much that hasn't been said!"

"Ten," she murmured.

"Ten?"

"Six."

"Will you marry me?"

"*Yes!*"

Sylvia Reichman

THE STREETS OF THE CITY

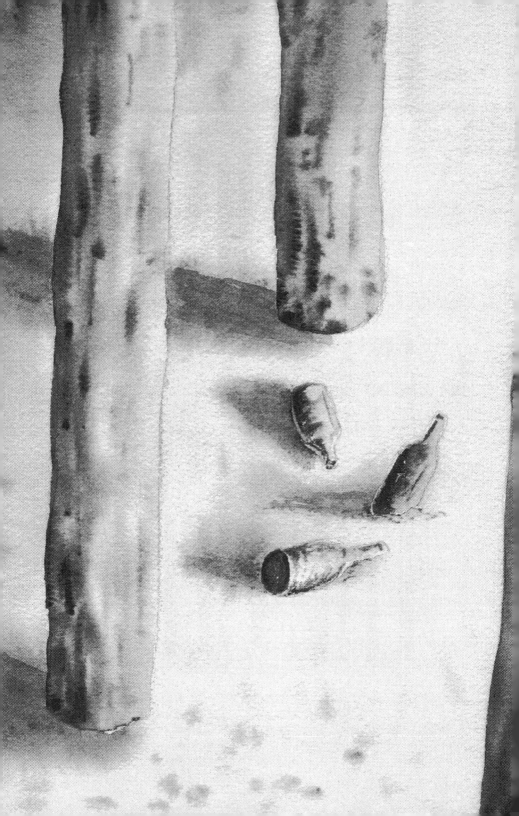

Land of the Free

From their bench, Buzz and Little Joe take in the activity of boardwalk life.

"A little of everything, eh?"

Buzz nods.

"Yeah, summertime in Venice Beach."

"Sure beats summertime in Vietnam."

"Let it rest, will ya? It's history."

"We shoulda won."

"Yeah, right...sleepin' under the pier?"

"Got a bottle?"

"Most of one."

"Let's go."

Steve Kelly

On the 5:25 Suburban

He sat facing her.

"I got fired today. They said I'm unstable."

She sat there silently. He turned away, looking at the slanting rain. His lips trembled.

"Nobody seems to care," he said.

Later at dinner, her friend asked, "Anything wrong?"

Her fingers danced as she signed: "That-man-on-the-train. He-looked-upset."

Mark Cohen

Headed for Trouble

The scantily clad hitchhiker knew she was in trouble the moment she stepped into the car.

The driver gazed disapprovingly at her costume. "Looking for some fun?"

"No...I'm just going to the beach."

"Think so? Well, I've got other plans for you, sweetie, and they don't include beaches."

"Guess I'm grounded, huh Mom?"

Dick Skeen

Gratitude

The street lights were a warm welcome from the oncoming chill of darkness.

The park bench's curvature felt familiar under his tired old spine.

The wool blanket from the Salvation Army was comfortable around his shoulders and the pair of shoes he'd found in the dumpster today fit perfectly.

God, he thought, isn't life grand.

Andrew E. Hunt

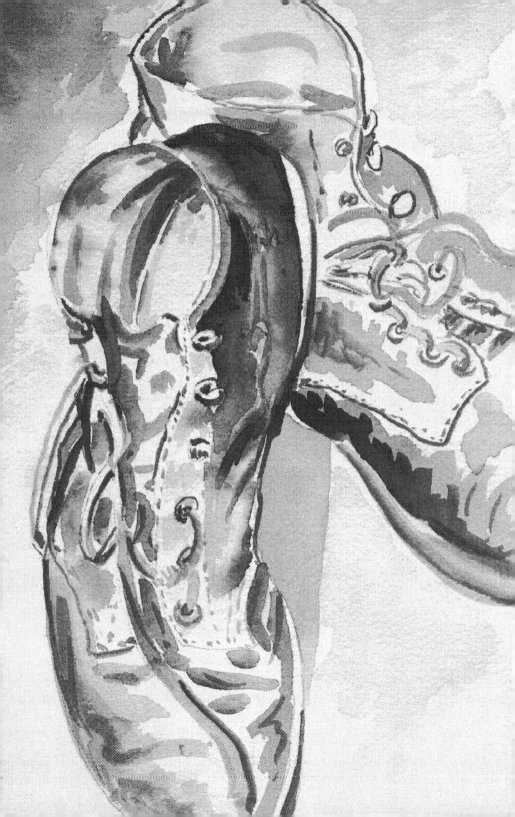

In the Bar

"Take the bimbo on the end."

"No...I don't want her."

"Why not?"

"She's obviously the reject."

"Why do you say that?"

"I don't know."

"You think she deserves more?"

"Yes."

"Really?"

"Definitely."

"Being over forty is harder than I thought."

"No, it hones a person's tastes."

"What if I take her, then?"

Emily Tilton

Distressed

They say evil wears no face. Indeed, there was no emotion on his face. No flicker of empathy as he inflicted still more pain. Couldn't he see the terror in my eyes or the panic on my face?

He calmly, even professionally, continued his dirty work, and then glibly spoke: "Rinse, please."

Dan Andrews

Patrol

On a side street he sat, continuing his nightly vigil.

With the dome light on, he read the headlines of the newspaper propped against the steering wheel. The radio blared, calling his number. The dome light went off, replaced by the red and blues.

Hoping not to make headlines himself, he pulled into the night.

Timothy Graf

Late Snack

Billy the burglar enjoyed short working hours.

Early one morning he crawled beneath a barrier to enter a house. He removed small, valuable articles and piled them in his car.

His last trip inside was for a snack in front of the television where he fell asleep in the tented, soon-to-be-fumigated house.

Dolorez Roupe

The Million-Dollar Party

With his last dollar Charlie won the $10,000,000 lottery. The celebration that followed with his street friends lasted two weeks, during which Charlie died from over indulgence.

The state claimed his millions, but his name will live forever on Main Street as the greatest party-giver ever known.

...What *was* his name?

Dick Skeen

Just
One Take

"Idiot!" The location director screamed at the prop master. "Can't you remember *anything*? Now we'll have to use real beer in the shot."

The aging actor seated at the downtown bar selected for this, the film's final day of shooting, looked down at his trembling hands.

Pray for 20 takes, he thought.

Dean Christianson

Revelation

Of all the video games in the arcade, Richie liked Quark Invaders best.

But on that Saturday morning, as he casually destroyed galaxies and vaporized planets, the troubling realization came to him that his success in life would probably not be predicated on how well he coordinated his eyes and killing thumb.

Raymond Abney

The Ordeal

She hated them! All of them! Their masks hid not their glee, as their groping hands held her down—for him.

The pain and blood were unbearable. Still, he persisted, forcing her.

Her screams only encouraged him. She knew not to deliver meant certain death.

Finally, satisfied, he said, "It's a boy."

Tom McGrane

No Words Left

Alzheimer's was killing his father. He held the door at the restaurant as his father shuffled in for Sunday breakfast. An older gentleman inside helped, whispering, "You're a good boy" to the son.

After his father died, he always remembered those words, knowing his father would have said them himself if he could have.

E. Karl Foulk Jr.

Losin' It

He was almost 23 and still a virgin. All of his friends kidded him because they had done it many times. So midnight one Friday he decided to put an end to it. Shyly, he approached the window and handed the girl behind the glass his money.

"One for 'Rocky Horror,'" he said.

David Hofman

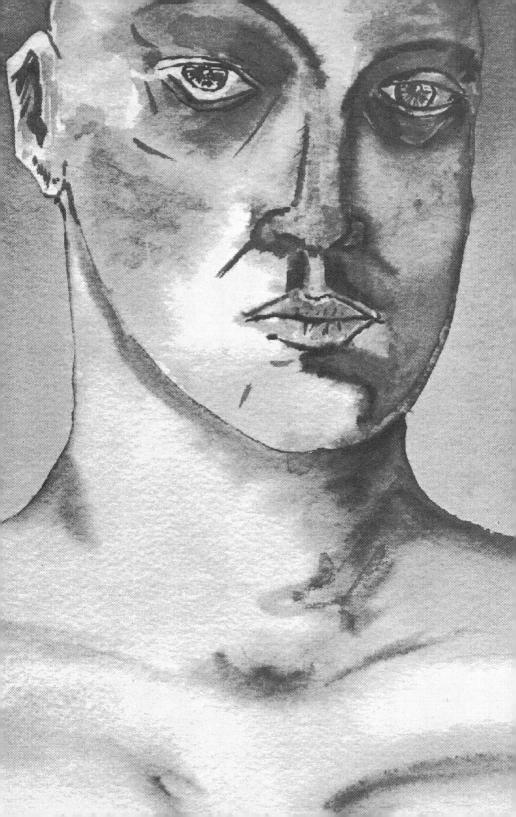

It Was a Year Ago

A slight breeze blew as Doug stood staring down at Joey.

"Hello, Joey," said Doug.

Silence surrounded the two of them.

"Joey, I'm sorry. I didn't mean it. I didn't. And, Joey—Merry Christmas."

Doug placed a rose on Joey's tombstone and walked away.

"Can you ever forgive me," he asked, "for driving home drunk?"

Grace Caguimbaga

El Muerto

I feel cold in this darkness.

Earlier tonight a delivery on a dark road would earn me $5,000 for a short night's work.

Paco was there, but something went wrong.

I am out in the glaring light. A man in white reads my name from a tag on my toe. I cannot answer.

Tom Odencrans

Hide and Seek

At last he would really show them. He'd picked the very best place to hide. They'd all say he could play the game better than anyone. When they found him, they'd clap their hands.

The dopes. How dumb can they get? They should have looked here first! It's so obvious!

Here in the abandoned refrigerator.

Douglas L. Haskins

Sober Intelligence

I watched some fool stumble out of the bar and into a car. When he swerved down the road, I pulled him over and administered a field test that proved nothing.

He requested a blood test; there was no alcohol in his blood.

"What's your game, pal?"

"I'm the D.D."

"Designated Driver?"

"Designated Decoy."

Sage Romano

Here Now

They did it in the office next to the taco stand. Small things meant a lot: a flower in a plastic cup, the lost shoes, the picture of Jesus.

"We're going to pray for you now, Billy," they repeated.

Tongues of cold fire. Exorcism. Mind rape.

"Remember," Billy said nine hours later. "Remember the terror."

Michael Julian Phillips

Vox Populi

"Hello. You have reached 891-4207, the Johnson residence.

"Mary and Jim are not living here during their custody dispute. If you're a creditor, please contact the U.S. Bankruptcy Court.

"Mary's analyst—when back from vacation—please call her at her mother's. To speak to Amy and Becky, press star.

"Have a great day."

Tom Ford

Getting to Know You

"I'm going to help block the clinic tomorrow," Judy told Tammy excitedly.

Her best friend looked surprised. "I'm going to the clinic tomorrow, too."

"Great! I'll pick you up!"

"No," said Tammy. "No...I don't—I really don't think that's such a good idea."

Her eyes filling with tears, she turned away from her friend.

Scott Long

Autumn Sonata

An October night. Rams on the tube. Cold cuts and beer for the guests, who banter about football and food.

Three hours ago, we buried my cousin, 23, needle-tracked arms and all. Hail Marys all around. Now the roar of the crowd drowns the gathering. The autumn moon will soon go down.

Robert F. Huttle

The Truth Is Found

The truth is found in curious places. In a bar, a drunk was espousing what he believed true.

Another drunk responded, "Belief comes before truth."

Beer glass held high, he continued, "I believe by dropping this glass, it'll break. To know the truth, I must let go."

To the bartender's displeasure, truth was revealed.

Michael W. Taylor

Harry's Love

He looked at her lying there, entranced by her sensuous curves, her golden glow. But it was her voice that really moved him—sometimes soft and sexy, sometimes wild with abandon. Whatever his mood, she matched it.

He lifted her lovingly to his lips. Tonight they would make beautiful music together, Harry and his trumpet.

Bill Horton

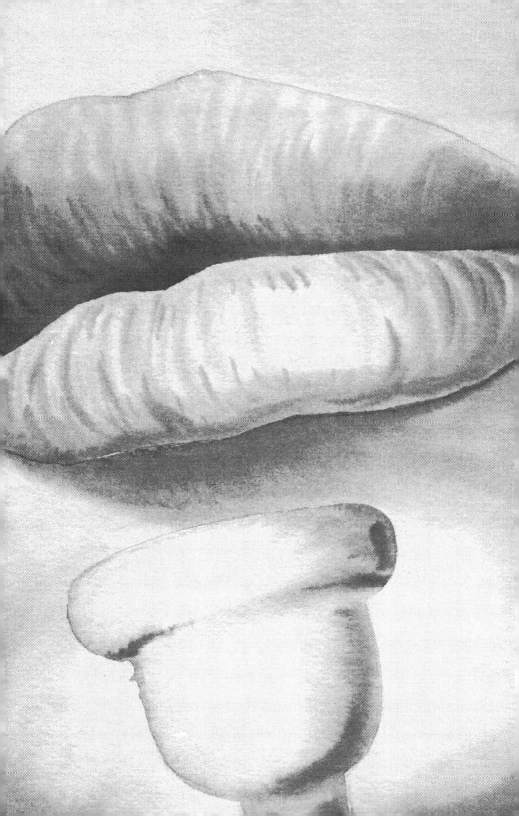

The Promise

"I'm opposed to it. It's wrong."

"Lying there relying entirely on tubes, drips, and pumps is right?"

"She's alive."

"And our promise to let her die with dignity?"

"But she gave us *our* lives!"

"Then we owe her dignity in death."

"Yes...I suppose...dear God..."

The night wind blew.

"Doctor, my brother and I—"

Lewis A. Henbury

The Demise of Old Customs

"...So I say, 'Lady, open your camera.' Sure enough, no film. String of undeclared pearls—"

"Excuse me, Chief. What about these big wooden crates from Nagoya, Japan?"

"Hands off! Those go directly to Canaveral. Word from upstairs."

"Yer the boss."

"Anyway, so I say, 'Lady, if we let every tourist carry in stuff like this—' "

Lach MacDonald

Higher Education

"College was a breeze," Jennings said, washing his grimy hands. "With all those budget cuts, they couldn't teach much. They just gave us our grades and sent us on our way."

"How did you learn?"

"We didn't, but so what? Look at me now."

A nurse opened the door.

"Dr. Jennings, you're wanted in surgery."

Ron Bast

The Deal

The CEO's office was plush indeed. The briefcase was genuine elephant leather, its contents 100 percent pure. The asking price a cool one mill.

The buyer inspected the goods; the seller inspected the cash.

On the street below, a whore talked to a john.

The buyer inspected the goods; the seller inspected the cash.

Thomas Quintana

Typecast

"**M**an, I'm *really* pissed off!"

"Why? What happened?"

"Some college kid. You know—buzzed-head-rap-music-neon-shorts-and-shades kinda guy."

"Yeah, I know the type."

"Anyway, this little yuppie dork asked me for a hooter! Can you believe it?!"

"That figures! Those jerks always judge people by the way they look."

Carne Lowgren

A December Story

Nick DeSantos, mailman, scanned the dead letter bin. Hundreds of envelopes bore the same address: "Santa Claus, North Pole."

"Hate seeing disappointed kids," Nick said to his supervisor.

"Serves 'em right," he said. "Believin' in Santa Claus."

Arriving home, Nick reached inside his bag and took out one of many letters.

"Dear Bobby," Nick wrote.

Dean Christianson

Daddy's Home

"Mommy? When's Daddy getting here?"

"Soon, very soon," she said. "The war's over...no more worrying."

"Mom, look—the boat's here!"

A ladder dropped down. Eventually, everyone was unloaded. Her husband Peter came ashore.

"Sign here," the lieutenant said. Betty stood embracing the coffin. "Peter... Why?" she asked.

Rafael Tobar

YONDER

Mephistopheles, Whisky, and the Wretched Soul

Mephistopheles stopped at the crossroads and tipped his flask o' whisky. A banker strolled by.

"Ten bucks for your soul."

"Try a million and a private jet."

"Look pal. Avarice, extortion, wickedness, and infidelity—Ten bucks is a steal for your wretched soul. The Reaper won't be so kind."

"Thirteen. No less."

"Deal!"

Both grinned.

Sean Christopher Weir

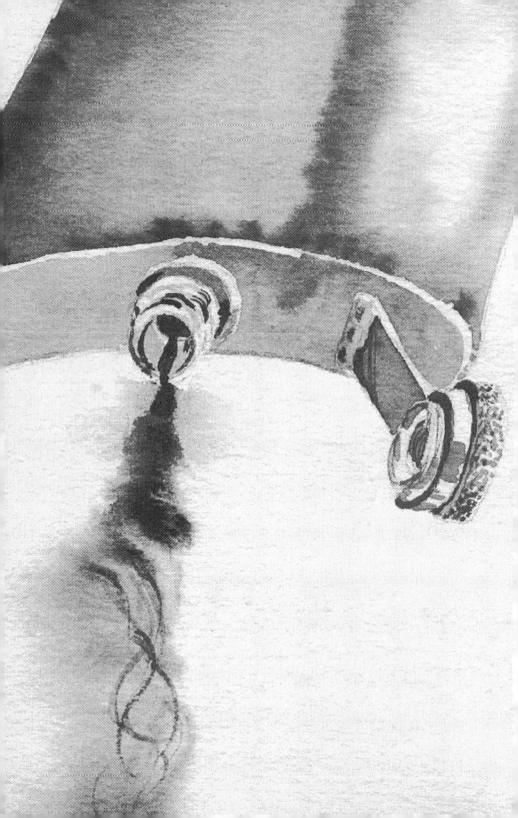

Honeymooners

The newlywed spider nervously walked back to the honeymoon web. Last night was fun, but this morning he noticed the red dot on her abdomen.

That afternoon, he said nothing while they drank medfly cocktails. She put an arm around him.

"You're awful quiet. What's eating you?"

The last thing he saw was flashing mandibles.

Christy Tillman

A New Life

Nine years, stranded on a forgotten moon of Uranus, the lone survivor of an interplanetary battle, I discovered intelligent, benign creatures who took me in and nurtured me. I learned from them, and grew to love them.

My people came for me at last. But we hid from the exploratory spacecraft.

Report: Gamma moon uninhabited.

August Salemi

English 1A

"Use a dash between coordinate elements containing commas."

My laser beam crackled out a response. One down.

"Subordinating clauses equal dangling participles."

I whirl and fire.

"I before eeeeeeeeeeeee—"

Two less mutant English teachers. More coming. Can't let them succeed. Teaching wrong us. Must them stop I. Modifiers misplaced. Metaphors mixing.

Over it's. Win they.

Rod Pound

Music Man

He's a music man, with notes drifting in and out of tune, eyes slitted from too much smoke, too little sleep.

Drunk on dusty melodies, he rides them to the edge of the sky, but the jukebox ears hear nothin'.

When "last call" comes, he'll dodge the grave and head for home again.

Robert F. Huttle

Wishful Thinking

Bob had all he wanted. And he still had one wish left.

"I can't decide. Can I use it later?" he asked.

"You da boss. I'm just the genie."

"Cool."

As he walked down the streets, he searched for a tune to express his joyous feelings.

"...Oh, I wish I were an Oscar Mayer wiener—"

Joshua Hanes

There's No Place Like It

The President was rushed to the Arizona desert to greet the arrival of the huge alien spacecraft.

"Peace," said the President.

"Thank you," said the very human-looking alien. "We've been on a million-year universal tour. We're excited about returning home."

"Please, visit. Then, good journey."

"No, you misunderstand," said the alien. "We *are* home."

Dean Christianson

Time for Armageddon

The day had finally arrived—God was angry.

The oceans overflowed with oil, the streets were filled with toxic waste, the pillaged rain forests caught fire and blazed uncontrollably.

God wadded up the Earth and flung it into the vast reaches of space.

"Time to start all over again," he said, grabbing a fresh planet.

D.L. Hanawalt

How the Chicken Got Its Reputation

"This suit's too *small*," croaked Buzzard. "My head sticks out!"

"Look at *me*," squawked Peahen. "Peacock got the colors! I demand new feathers!"

All the plain birds agreed, except Chicken, who was frightened. Angered, the other birds teased her, and she cowered more. But knowing no cuss words, they could only call her a chicken.

Terri Dunivant

Edmund's Discovery

Edmund's car wouldn't lecture him when he forgot to buckle up. The instant teller's cryptic note implied his PIN number didn't exist. The motion detector above the super-market door refused to notice him.

Troubled by these developments, Edmund sat in his empty apartment and thumbed reluctantly to the obituary column.

"I'll be damned," he said.

Paul Tucker

Dragon Tale

Muscles rippled under the blue-green scales as the dragon stretched, then relaxed.

Fascinated, I watched the creature freeze to perfect immobility. I stared until the man noticed me. With a glare, he rolled down his sleeve.

"Nice tattoo," I said, embarrassed.

"What tattoo?" he asked, turning away.

Under his sleeve, I saw something move.

Jana Seely

Perspective

"I think it's easy to see, my students, that by careful examination of these former inhabitants, of their behavior patterns, their simple, pointless lifestyles, the things they held of import, and of the complete and utter corruption of their selves and their environment, that Earth deserved no better than Galactic extermination. Thus, us. Any questions?"

Colin Campbell

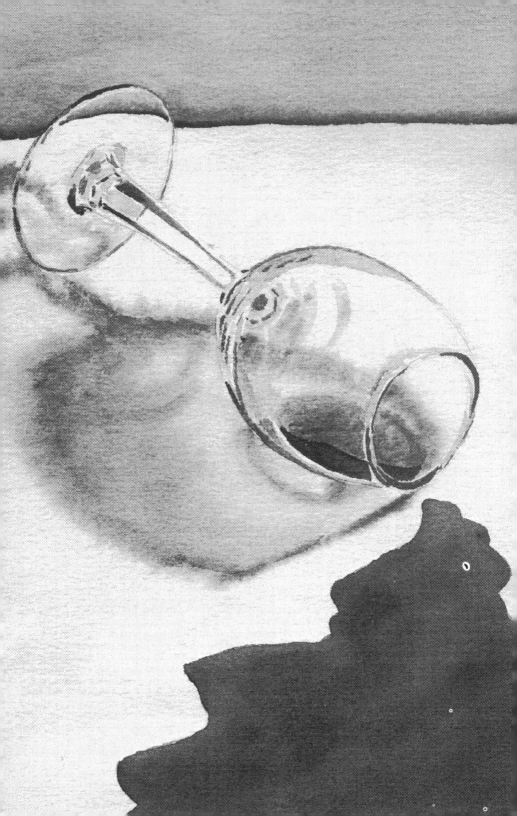

First Step

It's been three days since I've had a drink. Recently I learned about support groups. There's one for just about everything these days. I checked around and found a meeting.

Last night was the first time I had the nerve to stand up and say, "Hello. I'm Sandy, and I'm a vampire."

Maybe there's hope.

Tim Scott

Fat Teeth

To his horror, suddenly, inexplicably, the process reverses; his hamburger becomes a whopper, grows giant teeth through the relish, glistens menacingly with his own saliva, then begins a slow, contented counter clockwise grinding—eating *him* up!—until he becomes lost in meticulous mastication, washed down with his own Diet Coke and double order of fries.

Ray Clark Dickson

Communique

Uncontrolled terrorists burning the world's oil fields are producing "nuclear winter" effects in Northern Hemisphere.

Industry, agriculture, transport, failing. Prediction: 50 years until horse stock able to serve human needs. Gold, $2 an ounce. Hay passes $100 a bale.

U.S. denies plans to invade hay-producing nations.

"Just routine military maneuvers," says White House.

David Richards

The Bus Station

"One ticket to Hell please."

"I'm sorry, all departures going south are booked up."

"Anything else leaving tonight?"

"We have one bus heading in the opposite direction."

"Any seats available?"

"Plenty."

"Very long ride?"

"No, not really, but you might want to take a good book along. I've heard it's a mighty lonely trip."

Andrew E. Hunt

Population Control

The traffic moved past the "California Border" sign. Suddenly the sign began shaking violently. Then came a loud, rumbling roar.

"Earthquake!" people screamed as their cars braked sharply, turned around, and fled east from where they'd come.

In the underground operations room, a worker reset the computer controls labled *Signshaker* and *Rumble*...and waited.

Alan E. Mayer

The Visitation

Cecil sat up in his bed, roused by a ghostly slap through his face.

"Papa!" Cecil gasped.

"Don't Papa me!" Senior snorted from the mists. "You buried me in Jockey's! I'm supposed to bunch through eternity? Dig me up and do me right—*or you'll be sorry!*"

Senior was exhumed, redressed, and never seen again.

Andy Colberg

Oh, God

Set 'em up in this garden, see? Told 'em, "Don't eat the fruit."

Shoulda known. KA-BOOM! I kick 'em out.

But I'm a forgivin' kinda guy. Sheesh. Whadda sucker.

WHOOSH! I flood the place. Forty days, plus or minus. Dumb me. I save a couple.

What's their book say? Revelations? I gotta find a match.

Rod Pound

The Dying

The two policemen gazed down at him.

"Is he alive?"

"His eyes are moving."

"Won't be for long."

"Nope."

Staccato flashes climb a distant mountain.

"Poor guy."

"What's he looking at?"

"Couldn't tell you. Only he knows."

A little girl skips gladly before him, dropping an infinity of flowers.

Joe McCleskey

Art Vs. Commerce

The artist stood back to view the geometric precision of his latest creation.

"Beautiful," he murmured, "but will it sell?"

No time to examine the philosophic implications. Customers, buzzing with excitement, hovered near the piece. He wrapped up a deal quickly.

"This is business," the spider said with a vicious smile. "It ain't art."

Ron Bast

Guitar

He'll never hold me as he holds that guitar. Hasn't touched me that way in years.

I'll get inside the guitar, to be in his arms again.

She spent all day, sacrificing shape, voice, everything but desire to be held. Finally inside, mute, invisible, she waited.

"Honey, I'm home! I bought a new guitar! Honey...?"

John M. Daniel

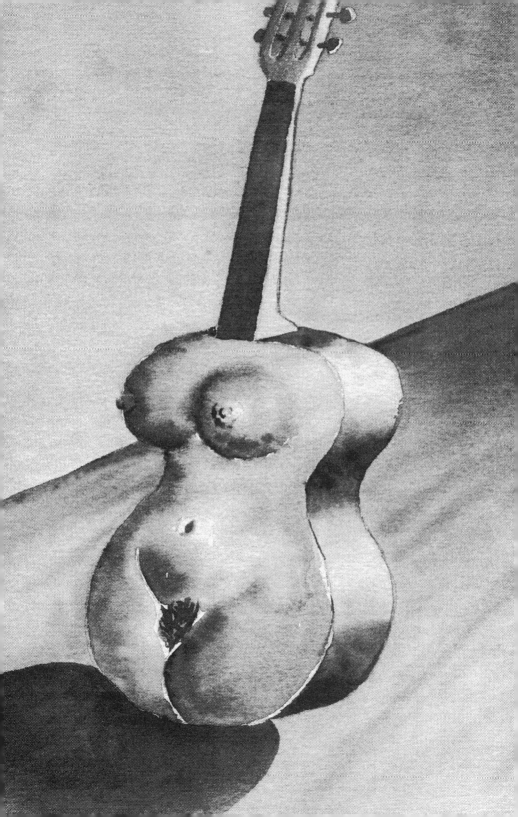

The Spaceman Cometh

"We are warriors. You are ready to join us—" said the alien to Mankind's ambassadors. Standing beside me, the general beamed.

"—Two thousand years ago, a prisoner, a pacifist, escaped to your world. We trust he did not disrupt your civilization."

From behind the general came a wail. A priest stood shaking, head in hands.

Dan Phillips

Typhoid Alex

Alex's talent was well-tested. The restaurant vanished the year after he stopped being a dishwasher. The school where he'd taught closed six months after his resignation. Shortly after he quit, the newspaper folded.

With a smile, Alex raised his hand and swore the oath making him a soldier in the United States Army.

Jane Mailander

Seeing Red

Those unblinking eyes!
I shouldn't feel this.
"Grandmother, your eyes..."
"Come." Her voice makes my legs yearn. "Give me a closer look."

I swoon. I dream of hunting horns, an axe, howling...

I awake. Grandmother's gone. Under her wet, red gown, the body of the finest animal I have ever beheld.

John M. Daniel

Strike Up the Band

"Hungry, my little majorette?" he puffed.

"Yes, Daddy! How much longer?"

"Soon...*Listen!*"

Daddy's digging was punctuated by the knell of midnight.

The spade struck wood.

He grinned, his teeth impossibly long in the moonlight.

"If you pick it clean, my little twirler, Daddy'll make the femur into a brand new baton."

Curt Homan

What the Devil Wanted

The two boys stood watching Satan walk away, the power of his hypnotic eyes still in their minds.

"Geez, what'd he want from you?"

"My soul. How 'bout you?"

"A quarter to call home."

"Oh. Wanna go get something to eat?"

"Yeah, but I can't. Now I'm out of money."

"No problem. I've got plenty."

Brian Newell

The End

"You didn't!"
"I did."
"Dead?"
"Yes."
"Why?"
"She knew."
"What?"
"About me."
"But what?"
"This."
"An alien!"
"Indeed."
"What now?"
"Now you."
"Oh, no!"
"Oh, yes."
"But why?"

"Because you know."
"But I won't—"
"Too late."
"—tell—"
"Far too late."
"—*anyone!*"
"Indeed."

"...Commander."
"Yes."
"Phase One has been completed."
"Excellent. Proceed with the invasion."
"Indeed."

Charles West

FURTHER
VOICES

Bad Luck

I awoke to searing pain all over my body. I opened my eyes and saw a nurse standing by my bed.

"Mr. Fujima," she said. "You were lucky to have survived the bombing of Hiroshima two days ago. But you're safe now here in this hospital."

Weakly, I asked, "Where am I?"

"Nagasaki," she said.

Alan E. Mayer

The Reunion

In school, she had been the closest thing to a girlfriend he ever had. "Please keep in touch," he said when they graduated. "Yeah, you too," she said. This reunion would be the first time they would talk in five years.

"Good to see you."

"Yeah, you too."

"Please keep in touch."

"Yeah, you too."

David Hofman

Equal Rites

"Highly irregular," said the priest.

"The diocese allows them," replied one of the men.

Overcoming a visceral dislike of same-sex unions, the priest agreed to hold the ceremony quietly. There was a harpist. Both men wore tuxedos.

But the priest, even while donning her vestments, still wondered if she was doing the right thing.

Mark Plants

Mislaid Plans

A rash of new bills came that morning. The letter from their insurance company announced the cancellation of their policies.

She sighed and rose wearily to tell her husband. The kitchen smelled of gas. On his desk she found the note.

"...the money from my life insurance will be enough for you and the children..."

Monica Ware

The Fall of a Legend

For a thousand years the mighty redwood grew into a majestic beauty, surviving earthquakes, fires, and drought. Outlasted only by the mountains on which it lived. A thousand years untouched. A thousand years unconquered.

"How long ta drop it?" shouted the foreman.

"Couple hours tops," spat the burly logger.

"Let's get it over with."

Andrew E. Hunt

Death of a Neighbor

My neighbor died yesterday. Roberta was a large woman with auburn hair I admired.

Though a private person, she was passionately interested in me. Her adoration confused me. I barely knew her.

After the funeral, Roberta's nephew handed me an inscribed hatbox. It read: "For lovely Catherine—my auburn wig. Your neighbor, Robert Whiting."

Mary Young

At the Hospital

"She needs surgery. It's a rare kind of tumor."

"Has anyone told her?"

"No. We're waiting for her family."

"There is no family."

"Everyone has family."

"Not her...what are her chances?"

"Not good. Only fifty-fifty."

"Those are good odds for her."

"They are?"

"They are."

"How so?"

"She arrived here an attempted suicide."

Emily Tilton

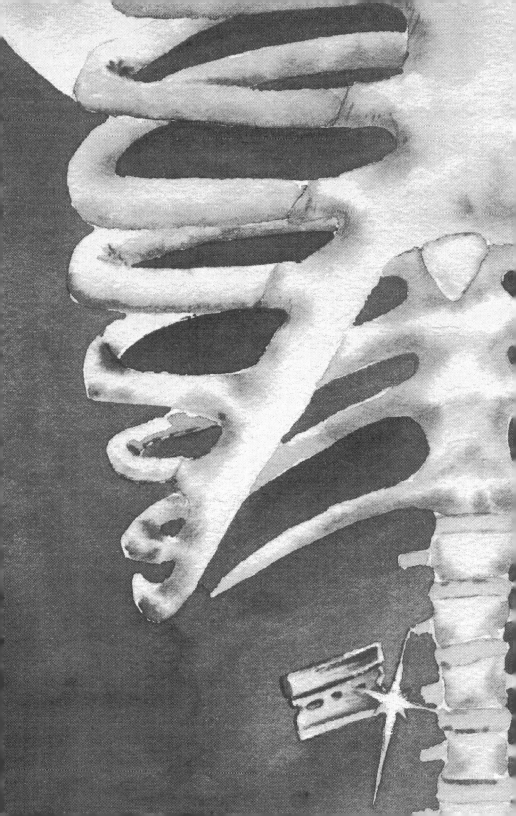

The Forest

Deep in the woods, trees filled the sky. On an incline, I turned to see the white-tailed buck gracefully bound toward the ridge.

Grandmother had called this The Season of Deer Rutting. Seeing one pass meant you'd travel soon.

I left in the morning fog, amid sounds of rifle fire. Deer season had begun.

Merrylyn Reynolds-Archambo

That Donna

Approaching her mother's front door was always difficult. But today Sharon thought she might finally get approval. Married, respectable (unlike her sister, Donna!), she was pregnant with that first grandchild her mother so longed for.

The door burst open, revealing her mother's beaming face. Could she already know?

"Sharon! Sharon! Donna's going to have twins!"

Bonnie Gartshore

War Game

Corporal John Thomas cowered in the mud as the unreal violence of his first combat exploded around him.

"Johnny!" His mother's voice echoed above the sound of battle. "It's time for dinner!"

Tears in his eyes, Corporal Thomas dropped his M-16 and ran toward the voice.

A machine gun chattered briefly, then fell silent.

Ron Bast

Maid to Serve

"He likes dinner at six sharp," she cautioned the new maid. "And absolutely no beef. He takes dessert in the den. Draw his bath at eight, he retires early."

"And when will I get to meet the master?" the maid asked as she stumbled backward over a sleeping poodle.

"You just did," laughed the housekeeper.

Emily Tilton

A Cowboy Movie

Jack's father died. The machines confirmed it. The nurse entered the room, started unplugging equipment. "You can go now," she explained.

He felt like he was in a theater. The lights were on. There was gum and popcorn on the floor.

"Dad," he almost said, "let's go."

Instead, he just watched the credits roll.

Ernest M. Garcia

All at Sea

Her quick footsteps overhead awakened him. Fearful of passing ships, she'd slept on deck. Her caution irritated him; they had quarreled bitterly.

He heard the splash. Ignoring her screams for help, he turned his radio louder. Then he wondered what had alarmed her.

The huge tanker came swiftly, on collision course with the little sloop.

Rosemary Manchester

Four
for Dinner

The oven door slammed shut with a loud, distinctive bang. The souffle quivered momentarily, then fell flat.

In the dining room, the prospective in-laws scraped their chairs back from the table, gathered up their wooly wraps, their precious son, and left in a huff.

Samantha smiled. The two cats smiled. The wedding was off.

J. Brechler

The Caretaker

"Don't walk on the grass!" shouted the little man.

"Don't be stupid," the large man replied. "It doesn't feel anything."

"You must care for it," retorted the little man. "It gives us beauty, but it's fragile."

"Whatever." The large man walked away.

Years later, each had moved on.

Indifferently, the cemetery grass grew over both.

Steven MacLeod

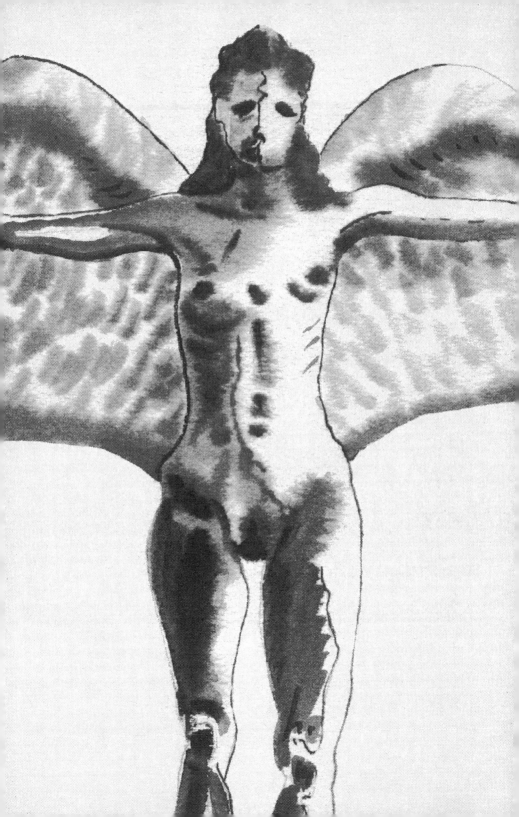

Last Flight

On a Greyhound bound for the Grand Canyon, she traveled unnoticed among the tourists, but carried no luggage or sensible shoes.

The driver slowed, announcing, "Scenic overlook ahead."

Passengers unloaded, fumbling for binoculars and cameras.

She stepped close to the edge. It had gone on long enough. Fight or flight? Fight or flight?

Flight.

Wendy Liepman

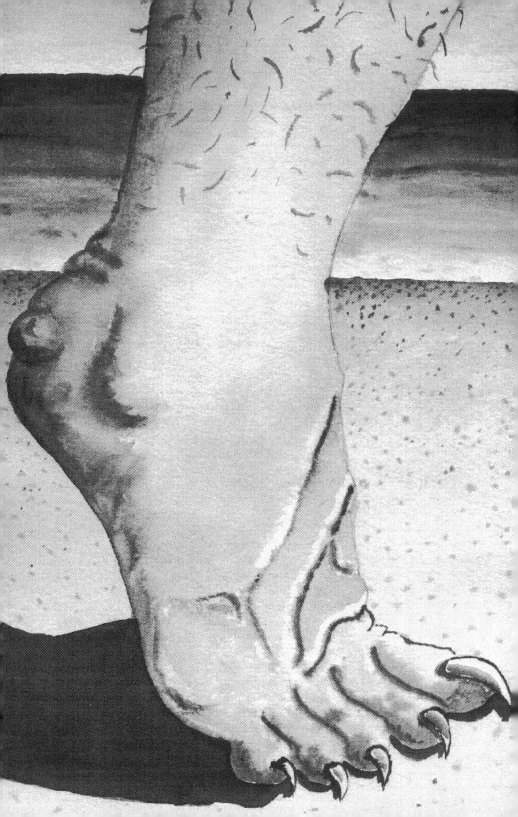

Footsteps in the Sand

Down on the hard, wet sand, a man raced past, disappearing into the night fog. Their eyes followed him, then turned to watch for his pursuer.

"Just his own demons, I guess."

"Got any yourself?"

"Just you, sweetie."

"He'll run out of beach...or breath."

"Or, hopefully, demons."

"I guess it's always a race."

Ross Parsons

In the Rough

Chip was teed off.

He'd never shot an eagle. Lots of birdies in his day, but never an eagle.

He sliced it accidentally.

Chip wanted no pared of this, putt he hooked himself in a trap.

His sentence? Behind the irons. Thrown in the bunker for eighteen hole years.

A bogey in society's nose.

Ran Swanson

Learning Curve

I was leaning against a used car when this red Pinto pulled onto the lot beside me. An elderly woman peered out.

"Do you discount here?"

"Yes, ma'am!" I said, containing my excitement.

She started leaving. "Pappy always said there's no bargain in discounted goods."

I lost a customer, but gained a point of view.

Jimmy Evans

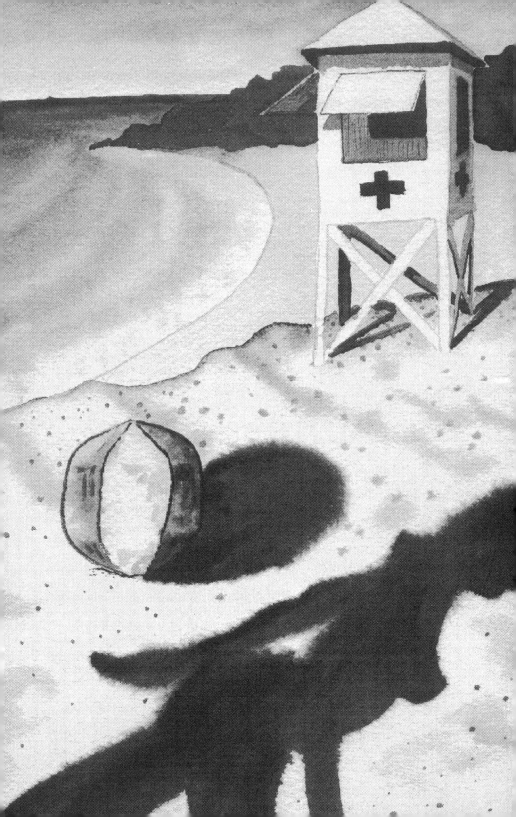

Fair Play

Irv and Ivan lay on the blistering sands, ogling women.

"That one?" Irv asked.

"Nope," Ivan said. "Too fat."

"Her?"

"Nope, too skinny."

In the warm sun they sipped beer and gawked.

"Wow," said Ivan. "Look at her!"

Two girls, wearing flaming pink bikinis, glided past.

"Nope," they heard one say to the other.

Fred W. Manzo

Dentist's Theater

The observers waited in anticipation. His heart beating furiously, he opened the beast's mouth. Against its dark gums its teeth gleamed whitely. He began to polish them, first gently, then with increasing energy. The demonstration was going well; the spectators recognized his skill and murmured favorably to one another.

Then he missed an E-flat.

Mark Plants

Love of His Life

When I saw the bearded lady at the carnival, I was determined to woo her. Such was my fetish, yet my relatives were supportive.

"Your name?" the minister asked of me.

"Robert Cedric Foster," I said. It all seemed too good to be true.

"And yours?" he asked of my bearded bride.

"William Angelo Duvani."

Wilmar N. Tognazzini

Chameleon Schlemieleon

The Brainiac. The Nerd. Not anymore. A midsemester move to a new school. A chance for a new identity.

Algebra. First day. First period. Sitting in the back with the cool people, hoping to clique, I finish my exam long before anyone else.

Doubting my calculations, the teacher grades it aloud: 100.

I've failed.

Patrick S. Tray

Harold
and Catherine

Catherine went through many men before she found Harold, a heavyweight boxer who shared her passion for raspberry Jell-O.

But one night as she was sitting at ringside eating her Jell-O and watching Harold pulverize the face of a journeyman pug, she realized sometimes life imitates art, and she was suddenly no longer hungry.

Raymond Abney

Grapplemeyer

"Old Grapplemeyer died broke. The reading of this will is over."

"That old fraud," sobbed Lydia, Grapplemeyer's mistress of 30 years. "I've wasted my life."

"You?" shouted David. "I was his secretary, valet, and more!"

"I was only the cook, but I'll miss dear Mr. Grapplemeyer," said Rosemary, fingering a huge diamond ring.

Shirley Powell

Care for Another Bite?

The animal's brown eyes peered at Tom, full of innocence and trust. Without remorse, Tom placed the gun between those eyes and pulled the trigger. As he butchered the animal, he thought of sizzling steaks.

Later, he savored a mouthful. As the well-marbled meat slid down his throat, the animal began its own revenge.

Brian Barnes

Lost

"My kids!" she screamed, rifling underneath clothes racks, where they sometimes hid.

Shoppers stared.

"Help me! They're gone!" she cried.

Someone whispered, "...old lady thinks—"

"Old!" she exploded, "I'm only—"

She froze. Her eyes shifted from face to face, from confusion to shame, then drifted to her own wrinkled hands.

"My...kids," she mumbled.

Nancy Ruth Nerenberg

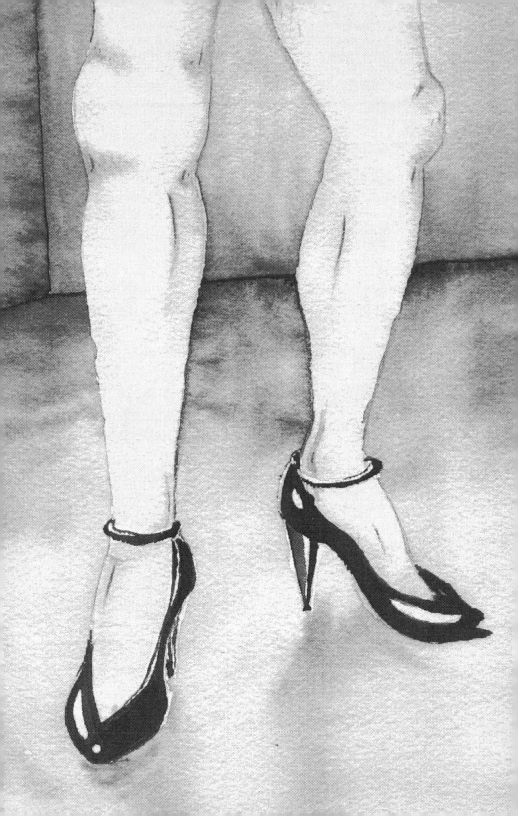

Evening Surprise

Shimmery stockings stretched over shapely thighs—a perfect backdrop for a body-skimming cocktail dress. Glamour radiated from the ends of the diamond earrings to the tips of the spike-heeled shoes. As a shadowed eye surveyed the mirror's reflection, painted lips pursed with pleasure. Suddenly, a voice cried out from behind.

"*Dad?!*"

Hillary Clay

Fate

This was the only way, such a blur of rage and bliss and hurled toasters as our time together had become. Appeal to fate: heads, we'd marry, tails, we'd separate forever.

The coin flipped, thudded, skipped and lay still, an eagle showing.

We stared as it sank in.

Then, together, "Best two out of three?"

J. Ripp

Sequel Time

The convertible flew over the cliff's edge into the deep desert canyon, finally hitting far below with a thunderous crash.

Two occupants crawled from the wreckage.

"Damn! Thank God for seatbelts!"

"And dual air bags! Jeez, what a mess!"

"I can't believe we made it! That was sure some shortcut!"

"Think we lost 'em, Thelma?"

Upton O. Good

Death in
the City

"He's begging, Father," the patrolman said.

"It's a fake collar, understand? I'm on my way to a goddam party."

Another moan from the man dying at our feet. He'd been struck by a driver long gone.

"Absolution, Father. I doubt he has time to read your credentials."

Kneeling and feeling foolish, I signed the cross.

H.W. Moss

June 12, 1994, 10:03 P.M.

"Jeez, O.J.—sometimes you startle me!"

"Aw, I'm sorry Nicole. I just can't seem to stay away."

"Well, beat it before I call 911."

"But I just wanna talk..."

"Not now—here's Ron with Mom's glasses."

"Hiya, Ron!"

"Hey, O.J."

"O.J. was just leaving, Ron..."

"Bye, Nicole. Call you from Chicago."

"'Night, O.J."

"'Night, Nicole."

Lach MacDonald

Solitaire

Encased by the laundry room walls, she stuffed load after load into the insatiable washer, begrudging every minute lost. Sodden diapers, mismatched booties, Batman pajamas, pink leotards, grass-stained soccer shirts, knee-socks, pinafores, jeans, sweaters, skirts, trousers.

Now, finally, she washes one small load a week, and wonders why the days are so long.

Marilee Swircszek

My Recipe for Writers Jam

I take one small brain, stuff it with plots and characters, add spice, a pinch of salt, mix in ideas, and put it on the back burner to simmer indefinitely. When ready to serve, I scrape off the mold, chop, process, and form to size. I offer this aesthetic delight, my friends, with relish.

Connie Suddath

55 fiction

THE RULES

How hard is it to write a 55-word short story? We bet you've been reading these stories and thinking to yourself, "Hey, I can do that. Give me a pen and paper."

We think you can, too, which is why we've included this handy dandy section of Official Fifty-Five Fiction Rules so you can know exactly how to go about it when the urge strikes.

But be forewarned: Writing a Fifty-Five Fiction story isn't as easy as it looks.

A haiku poem is short. So is a quarterback sneak. But nobody thinks they're simple to execute—it's just that the people who do them well make it seem that way.

Taking a great story concept and developing it within such a limited space is a little like carving a beautiful sculpture from a tiny block of wood. The working range is truncated and intimate, but the goal is no different than if you were creating on a much larger scale: to perfectly merge various elements into a coherent whole that ultimately makes people say, "Wow, that's really great!"

But don't be discouraged by such a lofty goal. Great storytelling starts with fair storytelling and gets better with practice. Ray Bradbury once told an audience that if they wanted to learn how to write, they should compose a short story every day. "If you do that," he said, "by the end of the year you'll have written 365 stories —and, at the very least, three or four of them are bound to be good because it's impossible to write 365 bad stories!"

We've often thought about that when judging our Fifty-Five Fiction Contest each year. It's the perfect way for someone to apply Bradbury's One-Story-a-Day Theory of Writing. When you've mastered 55 words, you can go on to 110, then 220, and so on until you've written that great novel that's been inside you, struggling to get out.

But we're getting ahead of ourselves. Fifty-Five Fiction is the name of this writing game, a tiny literary genre with a proud tradition stretching back a full eight years to a time when finding good copy to fill our arts and entertainment publication, New Times, was tough to do. Out of this necessity rose Fifty-Five Fiction.

The first rule we always tell Fifty-Five Fiction writers may seem obvious, but it's broken more often than you might think. We tell them to remember that we're talking about *fiction*, not essays or poems or errant thoughts. A lot of people have a hard time getting that straight, no doubt because they have a hard time believing that writing something so short is really possible. They usually end up with only part of a story, often with their character stranded in a situation going nowhere.

So although some may have a more complex definition of just what constitutes a "story," for our purposes, a story is a story only if it contains the following four elements: 1) a setting; 2) a character or characters; 3) conflict; and 4) resolution.

For those who think this limiting to their creativity, consider for a moment that:

• All stories have to be happening someplace, which means they have to have a setting of some kind, even if it's the other side of the universe, the inner reaches of someone's mind, or just the house next door.

• Characters can have infinite variations. People, animals, clouds, microbes. Anything.

• By conflict, we merely mean that in the course of the story, something has to *happen*. The lovers argue. The deer flees. The astronauts wait in anticipation. Even in this last example, something is happening, even though no one is moving or talking. There is conflict, which leads us to:

• The outcome of the story, known also as the resolution. This doesn't necessarily mean that there's a moral ("Justice is its own reward," "In the end, love triumphs"), or even that the conflict itself is resolved. It may or may not be.

But what it does mean is that when the story ends, someone has to have learned something. Tony found out his wife wanted to kill him after all; the soldiers successfully eluded the enemy when they thought they'd been discovered; Barbara was shown to be as much of a liar as her father. It's even possible to have none of the characters learn anything. But if that's the case, then we the reader must.

Consider "Bedtime Story" by Jeffrey Whitmore on page 15. Besides having a terrific story idea, Whitmore also goes about telling it well. How he does so is worth examining.

Notice how much he achieves through suggestion. We know the characters are lovers, but the author never says so. We also know there's a gun in the story, but it's never directly mentioned. In fact, Whitmore's tale is actually two stories. The second one— the other conspiracy—reveals itself in the final two words.

You'll also notice that there are no descriptive adverbs or adjectives, and yet we see the entire scene perfectly. The author then stretches the form by having his story start even before his narrative begins, and end beyond his final phrase, making it seem longer than just 55 words.

The main advantage to suggestion is conveying information economically—when the reader knows what you're talking about without your saying so, fewer words are needed. The disadvantage, of course, is losing sight of whether the reader is following you. Too much suggestion becomes obscure and confusing. That's a common error. So is trying to tell too complicated a story in such a tiny space. Fifty-Five Fiction demands a tight focus.

Telling a story in a traditional narrative mode is probably the best approach for new writers, but keep in mind that Fifty-Five Fiction encourages experimentation.

Can an entire story be told with every word starting with the same letter of the alphabet? Sure it can. You'll find it on page 69.

How about revealing a family's ongoing woes through just an answering machine's message? Check out page 131.

And on page 31, lovers meet clandestinely and discover more than they bargained for, in a tale with only one sentence using almost all nouns.

Surprise endings are often found in Fifty-Five Fiction, but they're not a prerequisite for success. They probably turn up a lot because they're easy to work with, and because many writers instinctively aim for the impact of a twist at the end. H. H. Munro had similar instincts in his finely crafted mini-short stories. So did Rod Serling and Alfred Hitchcock in their famous half-hour TV programs. Pretty good storytellers to emulate.

A few other important points to keep in mind:

• You can write about anything you like, but you can't use more than 55 words. Yes, you can use fewer if you'd like to, but we don't know why anyone would—don't shortchange yourself even more than we already have.

And what, exactly, is a word? Simple. If it's in the dictionary, it's a word.

• Hyphenated words can't count as single words. For example, "blue-green dress" is three words, not two. Exceptions to this are any words that don't become two complete free-standing words when the hyphen is removed. Like "re-entry."

• Also, please note that your story's title isn't included in the word count. But remember that it can't be more than seven words long.

• Contractions count as single words, so if you're really seeking word economy (as you should be), keep this in mind. If you write, "He will jump," it's three words. But if you write, "He'll jump," it's only two. Very economical. By the same token, any contraction that's a shortened form of a word is also counted as a full word. Like using "'em" for "them."

• An initial also counts as a word (L.L. Bean, e.e. cummings, etc.) since it's basically an abbreviation of a full word. The only exception is when it's part of an acronym like MGM, NASA, or IBM. The reasoning here is that the wide use of these acronyms has in effect made them into single words.

• Remember that numbers count as words, too, expressed as either numerals (8, 28, 500, or 1984), or as words (eight, twenty-eight, etc.). But keep in mind our hyphenated-word rule. "Twenty-eight" is two words when written out, but only one when expressed as 28. Don't cheat yourself out of an extra word that you may need.

• Any punctuation is allowed, and no punctuation marks count as words, so don't worry about being miserly with them if they work to some effect.

There are a few clichés we suggest you avoid. Unless you can come up with really fresh takes on these old chestnuts, stay away from stories where the reader eventually discovers the protagonist is a cat (or some other animal); characters who appear to be having sex, but it turns out they're doing something innocent and mundane, and you just have a dirty mind; and any character who wakes up at the end and says, "Gosh, it was all a dream!" These go in the trash faster than the speed of light, as well they should.

So now that you've digested all the rules and you're putting all those great ideas of yours on paper, what are you going to do with the best ones after you've shown them to friends who all think you're brilliant? Good question. Here's a good answer. Send them to us so we can consider them for our next Fifty-Five Fiction book.

You can submit as many stories as you want, but remember that each story must be typed on its own sheet of paper. That means one story per page.

Make sure your name, address, and telephone number are included on each story, so we can contact you. This information needs to be with each one in case your stories get separated. Too many times, we've been unable to contact authors of great stories simply because they forgot this simple procedure.

So. If you think you've got some winning stories, put a stamp on that envelope and mail them off to us at Fifty-Five Fiction, Dept. 55, 197 Santa Rosa St., San Luis Obispo, CA 93405. Unfortunately, we can't acknowledge receipt of any work, so please send photocopies, not originals. If any of your stories are selected, one thing's for certain: You'll be hearing from us.

And remember: Just 55 words. Δ

Steve Moss

About the Editor: Steve Moss has always liked words—so much so that he decided to start his own weekly newspaper so if there was nothing around to read, he'd have no one but himself to blame. He studied art at Brooks Institute, UC Santa Barbara, and Syracuse University, but eventually switched to writing because journalists were more fun to hang out with. He's been a reporter, editor, busboy, art director, construction grunt, advertising copywriter, and graphic artist. He's the editor and co-publisher of New Times in San Luis Obispo, where he started Fifty-Five Fiction as an annual writing contest, and he can't imagine doing anything else. He now lives in Pismo Beach, Calif., with his hot tub.

About the Illustrator: After high school, Glen Starkey did a short, unsuccessful stint as a professional surfer before attending college as a professional student. Ten years later, he quit school after realizing there was no money in it and got into art, where the big bucks are. His paintings and drawings have been shown in numerous group and one-man exhibitions, and today he plies his trade as a professional illustrator, feature writer, and music critic. He's also a board member of the San Luis Obispo Art Center. He currently lives in San Luis Obispo, Calif., with his dog, Madison, who hasn't led nearly the illustrious life that Glen has.

About the Designer: Following his graduation from Cal Poly, San Luis Obispo, with a degree in graphic communications, Alex Zuniga helped found New Times. He's been its art director since Day One, even though at times he's had second thoughts. He's won awards and accolades for newspaper, poster, and book designs throughout his career, plays a mean game of basketball, whips up an even meaner barbecue, and makes his home in Los Osos, Calif., where friends are always just around the corner.

238